ROTHERHAM LIBRARY & INFORMATION SERVICES

This book must be returned by the date specified at the time of issue
as the DATE DUE FOR RETURN.
The loan may be extended (personally, by post or telephone) for a
further period if the book is not required by another reader, by quoting
the above number / author / title.

LIS7a

Today is Oscar's birthday.

Well, not really his birthday –

he's six months old.

The truth is, no one can

wait for his whole birthday...

"Dinosaurs and fairies"
For our Rosie, who knows about these things

First published 2005 by Walker Books Ltd, 87 Vauxhall Walk, London SE11 5HJ

10 9 8 7 6 5 4 3 2 1

© 2005 Blackbird Design Pty Ltd

The right of Bob Graham to be identified as author/illustrator of this work has been
asserted by him in accordance with the Copyright, Designs and Patents Act 1988

"HAPPY BIRTHDAY TO YOU" Words and Music by Patty S Hill and Mildred Hill
© 1935 (Renewed 1962) Summy-Birchard Music A Division of Summy-Birchard Inc.

Reproduced by permission of Keith Prowse Music Pub Co Ltd, London WC2H 0QY

This book has been typeset in StempelSchneidler

Printed in China

British Library Cataloguing in Publication Data: a catalogue record for this
book is available from the British Library

ISBN 1-84428-029-2

www.walkerbooks.co.uk

Oscar's Half Birthday

BOB GRAHAM

WALKER BOOKS
AND SUBSIDIARIES
LONDON · BOSTON · SYDNEY · AUCKLAND

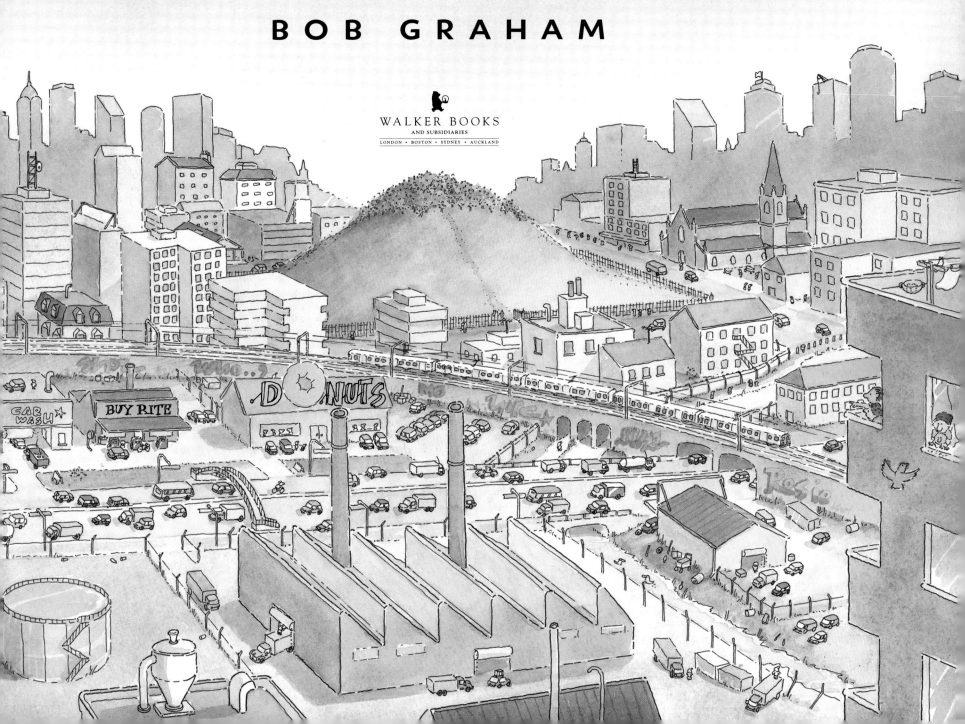

"Perfect day for half a birthday,"

says Oscar's dad.

The birthday boy waves his wet fists.

"And a picnic," says Oscar's mum.

Boris the dog raises one ear.

"With a birthday cake," says Oscar's sister, Millie.

She wears coat-hanger fairy wings

on her back and a dinosaur glove on her hand.

She's excited, and the dinosaur squeezes

Oscar's arm into soft little pillows.

"Careful, Millie," says Mum.

"A little more fairy and not so much

dinosaur," says Dad.

"But he's so CUTE," says Millie.

"I know," says Dad, and wraps

three tuna sandwiches in plastic.

"Where are we going?" asks Millie.

"The country," replies Dad.

"Well, not really the country," says Mum,

"up on Bellevue Hill."

"Half the country then," says Dad.

"For half a birthday," adds Mum.

In the lift, Millie the dinosaur presses all the buttons.

Bright as a Christmas tree they shine,

bright as candles on a cake,

glinting in Oscar's dark eyes…

They are a long time getting to the street.

They walk past the gasworks,
along by the factory gate
and across the footbridge.

High up over the traffic,
Oscar kicks his feet in the wind.
Millie's wings flap as Mum holds her tight.
Seagulls screech and bank off towards
the docks on the other side of the city.

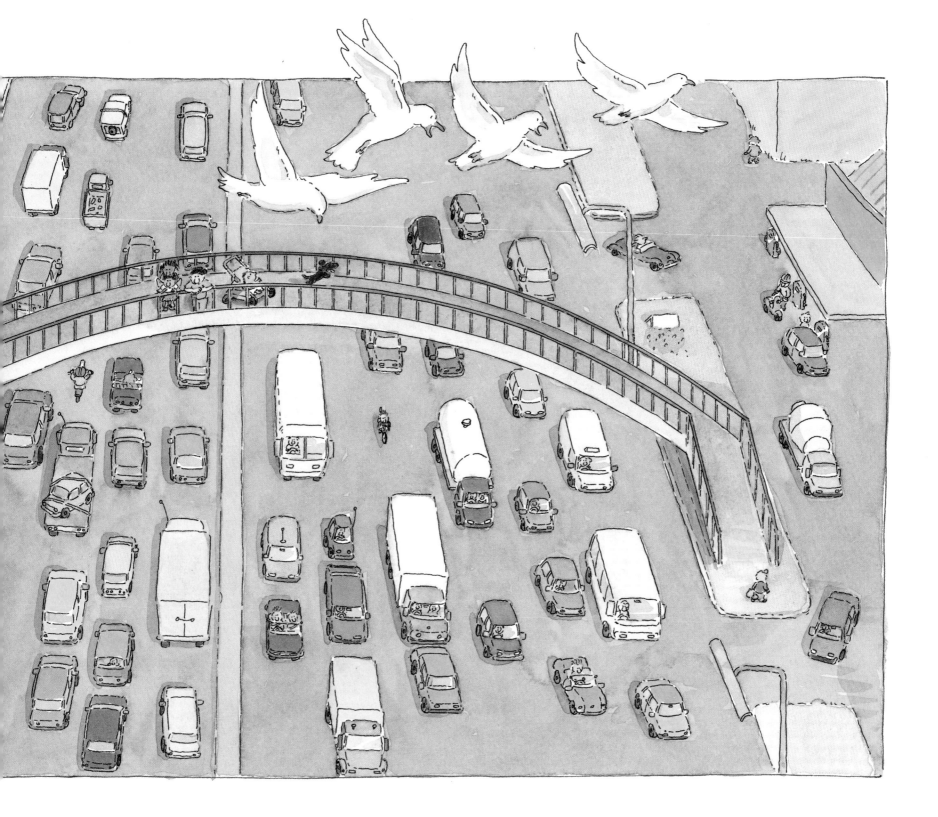

They push the pram slowly along by the canal,

wheels squeaking, Oscar waving, and stop in the tunnel.

There is a rushing of wind.

"HERE SHE COMES!" yells Dad.

Tickety-clack, tickety-clack, tickety-clack.

The eleven fifteen is belting down the track so fast

Millie can feel it all the way up through her pink sneakers.

"AND THERE SHE GOES!" yells Millie.

Tickety-clack, tickety-clack, tickety-clack –

fading away until all that can be

heard is the echo of water

dripping off the bridge,

plip, plip, plip,

into the canal below.

And at last they reach Bellevue Hill.

"Can we have our picnic now?" Millie asks.

"Well, let's find a nice spot first," says Mum.

"Are you hungry already?" says Dad.

"Yes," replies Millie.

"That's the dinosaur talking," says Mum.

"Not the fairy," adds Dad.

Millie the dinosaur grazes on
grass seeds stripped from their stalks
and Oscar falls quietly asleep
with his mouth open,
as they push on up the hill.

Near the top, the path goes through woods.
They listen to the wind in the trees
and the drone of distant traffic.
Boris chases rabbits.

Oscar frowns up against the light –
six different expressions on his face
in the time it takes a leaf to fall.